Cuthbert's Babies

Pamela Allen

Puffin Books

For William Thomas Hobbs Allen

One evening, before sleep, when Cuthbert was
cuddled up with his mother reading a story
she said, 'Cuthbert, would you like a baby brother?'
'No!' said Cuthbert.

In Cuthbert's family there was Cuthbert's mother, there was Cuthbert's father, there was Cuthbert's grandmother, there was Cuthbert's grandfather, and there was Cuthbert.

It had been like this for as long as
Cuthbert could remember
and he liked it just the way it was.

Then one day Cuthbert's mother and father
came home with not ONE baby boy
but FOUR darling little baby girls.

Everyone was there to welcome them.

There was a splendid afternoon tea.
'Isn't she pretty?' whispered Aunty Kitty.
'Look at her toes,' whispered Aunty Rose.
'Really? Fancy that,' nodded Great Uncle Pat.

'This little piggy went wee wee wee
all the way home,' sang Old Uncle Willy.
'Jenny dear, more tea?' asked Uncle Charlie.
'Bumble-boo-bum,' said Cuthbert.

After supper, Cuthbert wanted to play.

'Not now,' said his grandfather.
'I'm busy,' said his grandmother.

 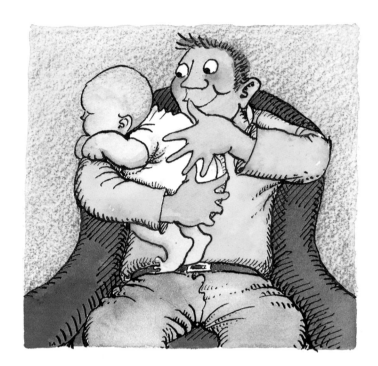

'Soon,' said his mother.
'You'll have to wait,' said his father.

But Cuthbert couldn't wait.
He felt BAD!
'I'll run away!' he shouted.
But nobody took any notice.
'I'm leaving!' he cried.
But nobody was listening.

In his room he still felt bad.
'Nobody loves me,' he whispered.
Then, shutting his eyes tight, he made a wish.
He wished with all his might for a boy to play with.
'Just like me, a BIG boy, a big BAD boy.'

Now out at sea three pirates slept
and in their dreams they heard his call.

They woke up and they rowed ashore,
Jeremy, Bellamy and Ted.

Then, creeping and crawling,
slithering and slipping,
through the damp and the dark they came.

'We're here,'
cried Jeremy.

'We're BAD,'
scowled Bellamy.

'We're BIG and
we're BAD,'
growled Ted.

So, stamping and stomping,
hollering and howling,
clattering and clomping,

for hours and hours they roared and they raved.

Oh, what a HULLABALLOO!

Then Jeremy said, 'We've brought the cannon.'
'Let's fire it,' said Bellamy.
'Yesss!' squealed Cuthbert in delight.
'We're BIG and we're BAD,' bellowed Ted.

'Now look what you've done,' said Cuthbert.

'Uh, oh,' murmured Jeremy.

'Listen,' whispered Bellamy,
'someone's coming.'

'We're going,' said Ted.
And down into the damp and
the dark they went.

'Don't forget your cannon,'
Cuthbert called.

Cuthbert tried to make the babies laugh.
He pulled funny faces, just like a clown.
He poked out his tongue and he jumped up and down.
But nothing he did would make the babies laugh.

Then Cuthbert's mother came.

'Oh dear,' she said.

So, one by one, on Cuthbert's bed,
she changed them and she fed them.

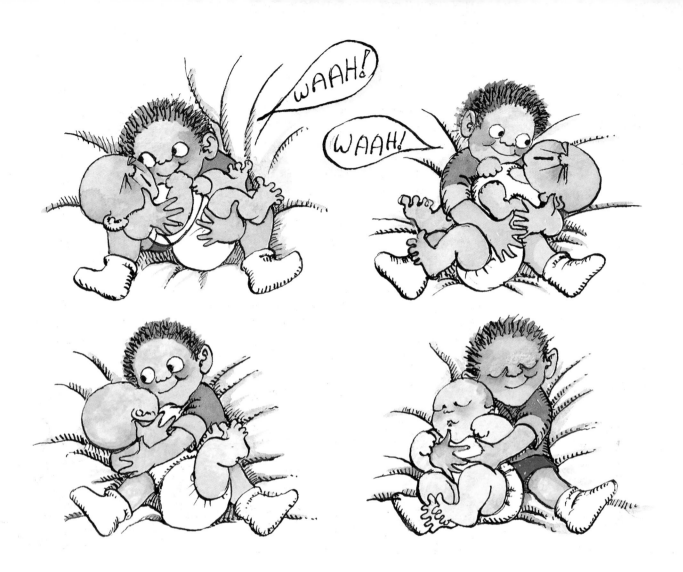

And, one by one, on Cuthbert's bed
he cuddled them and he comforted them,
until the crying stopped and they were
all fast asleep.

Then Cuthbert's mother wrapped each one firmly
and placed them in their own special bed.

'Time for our story,' she whispered.

She re-made Cuthbert's messy bed.
She helped him into his pyjamas.
She kicked off her shoes and climbed onto the bed.
'What will it be tonight, my beautiful boy?' she asked.
'The one about the pirates,' whispered Cuthbert
and he snuggled up really, really close – and smiled.